SOMERSET FOLK TALES FOR CHILDREN

SHARON JACKSTIES

The History Press

For Sienna and Lucia, for Cash, Theo and Maggie,
for Tommy and Darcy, for sand, sea and stories

First published 2018

The History Press
The Mill, Brimscombe Port
Stroud, Gloucestershire, GL5 2QG
www.thehistorypress.co.uk

British Library Cataloguing in Publication Data.
A catalogue record for this book is available from the British Library.

ISBN 978 0 7509 8480 5

Typesetting and origination by The History Press
Printed and bound in Great Britain by TJ Books Limited

CONTENTS

About the Author and Illustrator

SHARON JACKSTIES has been a professional storyteller for over twenty-five years. Passionate about the oral tradition, her interest in places and their stories also finds a voice in her teaching. Sharon runs courses at Halsway Manor in Somerset – England's only residential centre for the traditional arts – as well as abroad.

In 2016 she co-directed a new festival, the Summerlands Storytelling Festival, which spanned the South West.

Sharon's work with children started with her specialising in Theatre in Education and

working with the Unicorn Children's Theatre.
She lives in Somerset.

INTRODUCTION

I have been a storyteller for a very long time, telling stories from all over the world. Many years ago, I came to live in Somerset. As with any new place, I couldn't wait to explore. Moving to Somerset was like coming for the first time to an old, old house. An old house whose various rooms were like the different features and scenery in the Somerset landscape – with their own colours, shapes, sizes and even smells. Like the best houses with attics or cellars, I knew that there were secrets to discover, perhaps even treasure. So I went on a treasure hunt. The treasure I found wasn't what you could hold in your hand, or count like golden coins. It was stories. Like the best treasure, some of these stories are very old. They have been kept bright and shining by re-telling, re-reading and re-writing. Here is a riddle for you:

The more often you give me away, the longer you keep me. What am I?
The answer is at the back of this book.

Here is a treasure map of Somerset and the places these stories come from.

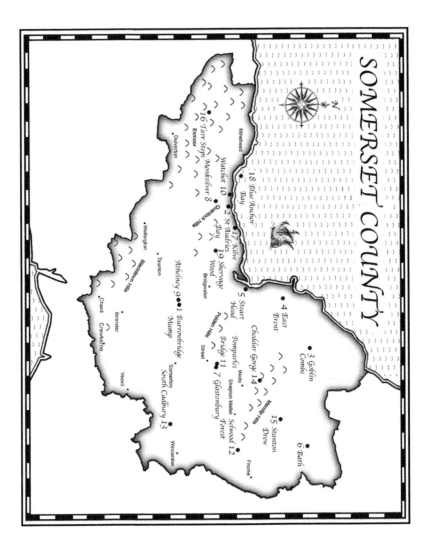

SOMERSET COUNTY

N

18 Blue Anchor Bay

17 Kilve

Minehead

16 Tarr Steps

Exmoor

Watchet 10

Montsilver 8

Quantock Hills

2 St Audries Bay

19 Sherwage Wood

Dulverton

Bridgwater

5 Steart Head

4 East Brent

3 Goblin Combe

Cheddar Gorge 14

Wellington

Blackdown Hills

Taunton

Athelney 9 ● ● 1 Burrowbridge Mump

Pompardis

Bridge 11

7 Glastonbury

Mendip Hills

15 Stanton Drew

6 Batch

Chard

Ilminster

Crewkerne

Yeovil

Somerton

South Cadbury 13

Wincanton

Wells

Shepton Mallet

Selwood 12 Forest

Street

Polden Hills

Frome

PART ONE

MAGICAL CREATURES

The King of the Moles

The River Parrett winds its way through the Somerset Levels like a great lazy snake until the rains come. They can last through autumn and winter and most of spring. Then the river loses its shape and hides beneath the vast lakes created by the floodwaters.

Near the banks of the Parrett is a small church with a chest in a cupboard in the vestry. Inside is an ancient altar cloth made out of moleskins. It is kept to remind people of one of the worst floods.

Not so long ago, the new lord inherited the big estate that sloped down to the river. Now that he was the new owner he wanted to change everything. When he had finished changing the great house, destroying old bits and adding new bits, he turned his attention to the land around it and decided that the avenue of 200-year-old oak trees looked rather untidy. Their branches were twisted in the wrong directions and when autumn came their leaves made a dreadful mess on the grass. As for the meadows, those slopes would look better if they were levelled off down to the river to make everything flat, and as for the river with all its untidy curves – they would have to be evened out.

He sent for the head gardener and gave instructions to chop, level and straighten. The gardener went pale with horror and warned him against it. The lord said that he hadn't asked for advice, he was giving an order. In time the work was done – there were no untidy trees on the horizon, the grass was completely flat and the riverbanks were as straight as a ruler. At last the lord was content, but only for a day. The next morning when he looked out on his empty landscape it had been spoiled by hundreds of heaps of dirty piles of earth. The moles had arrived, covering everywhere with their molehills. The head gardener had trouble hiding a smirk when the lord summoned him to give the order to get rid of the moles. Again he tried to warn his master, again he was overruled.

It took a long time to kill all those moles. So long, in fact, that all the fabrics on the estate and in the village were now made of mole skins: people slept on moleskin sheets, wore moleskin clothes and even the babies wore moleskin nappies. The local church boasted the only moleskin altar cloth that had ever been known in Britain.

At last the horrible task was over, there were no more molehills, the bare patches of earth had been reseeded with new grass and the lord was content. But only for a day. The next morning there were a few enormous piles of earth, far higher than any man. The head gardener didn't bother to hide his grin when he explained that the King of the Moles had arrived because he had heard that his people were in trouble. He was ordered to get rid of the King of the Moles but had to explain, whilst disguising his snigger with a cough, that there was only one person with that kind of skill, and as Micky-the-Mole was one of the travelling people, they would just have to wait until he happened to be passing. It was a long wait, during which the King of the Moles took his revenge by raising his massive piles of crumbling earth everywhere.

At last Micky-the-Mole was found sleeping in one of the few ditches that the lord hadn't ordered to be filled in. He was taken to the great house where the master stared at the strange man with dark velvety hair growing low over his face, a whiskery moustache offsetting huge yellow teeth, little piggy eyes a-blinking, a pink turned up nose a-trembling, and huge blunt hands swinging low like a pair of shovels. He was promised a bag of gold for the capture and killing of the King of the Moles, as long as the lord was able to see his tormentor before the giant mole was put to death.

In no time at all Micky-the-Mole was back, dragging an enormous cage. Inside was a mole the size of a calf. The lord was one of these people who believe that size isn't everything, but he had to believe the monster mole's gold crown, set with human teeth. He gave Micky a large bag of gold, told him to kill the beast in the cruellest way possible and come back to describe which method he had chosen. The sound of that cage, further weighed down with the sack of gold, scraping its way down the corridor, made the chimneys crooked and put cracks in the crystal chandeliers. But it was all worth it when Micky-the-Mole returned with the tale of the beast's death. The lord had spent a few delicious moments imagining the method. Had he been roasted slowly over a fire? Had he been skinned alive? Had he been drowned slowly on the riverbank as the tidal waters of the Parrett had risen? None of these was the case – the King of the Moles had been buried alive. The lord was so pleased at this cruellest of deaths that he

gave the killer an extra bag of gold. He was too cruel and too stupid to realise that as moles live underground, you can't kill one by burying it!

Soon after that the autumn rains came, heavier than before. It rained throughout the winter and the spring. There were no trees to drink it up, no slopes to protect the big house from the swollen river, no curved meanders to slow the flow. There weren't even any mole tunnels to soak up the extra water. The gardener splashed about with a moleskin umbrella and a huge grin, waiting for what must happen. The day came when the river became a foaming furious torrent, tearing through the first-floor windows of the house. The gardener was ready with a coracle – a small round river boat made with animal skin stretched around a frame made from willow withies. I bet you can guess what kind of skin it was. It also had a rowing boat tied to it. The last of the antique furniture and expensive paintings had been washed away, and the lord was swept along after them. The gardener grabbed him by his collar and hauled him into the coracle. When they were in the middle of the featureless flood, the gardener scrambled into the rowing boat, grabbed the oars and cut the rope. The coracle swirled away towards the sea with the lord still in it. The land had spat him out once and for all.

Sometimes you have to wait for the floodwaters to subside to reach Burrowbridge Mump. It rises like a great molehill in the flatness of the Somerset Levels. Inside, it is honeycombed with passages. Some people say it is a labyrinth, but locals know that these are mole tunnels made by the King of the Moles himself, spiralling around inside his castle. If you lay your ear to its slope when the moon is full, you can hear the chink, chink of gold pieces as Micky and the King share out their treasure.

THE SEA MORGAN'S SONG

If you go to the Somerset coast, there are parts of the shoreline that look like the surface of the moon, apart from all the water of course. Even the sea is strange, and, depending on the tide, seems unable to decide whether it is water or mud. The rocks curve in weird shapes and layers and the beach is joined by a waterfall that plunges down from the cliffs.

You can only reach the waterfall at low tide, which is when the Sea People, the Sea Morgans, pull themselves out onto the rocks, lashing their fishlike tails to help them crawl towards that fall of crystal-clear water. Living in the salty sea, it is a real treat for them to splash about in fresh water. Local people thought it was unlucky to disturb them and would always listen out for their singing, before venturing to that part of the beach themselves.

One night of the full moon, a fisherman was making his way to his boat when he heard them singing. They sounded so beautiful that he decided to stop and listen for a while. As he tiptoed over the moonlit beach, their lovely music wrapped him in their web of sound. The song seemed to become part of him and without realising, he began to hum along with it. Soon he was singing aloud with the Sea Morgans until they stopped abruptly. They had heard a voice they didn't recognise. Then there was a scrambling and a splashing, as terrified Sea Morgans desperately tried to reach the safety of the retreating tide.

Moments later the only sound was that of the waves. But then came another, so tiny at first that the fisherman wasn't sure that he had heard it – a wistful cry like a sea bird. It grew stronger and he didn't know if he was hearing crying or singing. Placed in the cleft of a rock to prevent her from rolling off, was a Sea Morgan's child. Apart from having too much hair for a human baby, she otherwise looked just like one, as she was still too young to have grown a tail.

She kicked her little legs and held out her arms to him and he picked her up as anybody would. Then he thought of his own baby who had only lived a few days before being buried in the little churchyard near the cliff top. Maybe that was why he didn't carry her down to the water's edge and leave her where her own people could reach her. Instead, he carried her home where his wife was overjoyed to have a baby to look after at last.

They called her Morgan, which means 'Of the Sea', and she grew up like and not like other children. They would put her to bed, but she would never seem to sleep. They could hear her singing strange songs to herself, and if they tiptoed past to look in on her, they caught the gleam of her sea-bright eyes and could see her rocking in the bed. Day or night, she was never still. Her thick wavy hair always felt damp and left sand on her comb and

pillow. In a single day her eyes could change colour from mud brown to grey, to blue and green. Perhaps because she was now living on land, she never grew a tail, but every moment she could she would be playing in water. She grew the way children grow without being quite like the other children of the village.

Unlike other girls, she loved to help her adoptive mother with the washing. Whatever the weather, she would be found swimming in the streams or the mill pond, and she sang more than she talked. People said that her voice was so lovely that the wind itself would stop blowing to hear her sing. They were glad to have her in the church choir until the day they found her splashing in the font where babies are baptised. That was when she was told she couldn't sing in the choir any more. The fisherman tried to get her to sit through the Sunday service instead, but without the singing to keep her happy, she wriggled and squirmed like a fish out of water. Before long she had slid off the pew and, bare feet slapping on the flagstones, she had run outside.

Disapproving mutters could be heard coming from the congregation:

'It would need a fishing net to keep that one still...'

'You'd have to catch her first...'

'What with, a harpoon?' came the cruel whisper.

The vicar quelled them with a hard look, but as they fell silent they could clearly hear Morgan singing joyfully outside, her single silver voice rivalling those of the whole choir.

When the villagers left the church, they found Morgan leaping from the horse trough into the mill pond and back again. Her clothes lay tangled by the edge of the pond like a heap of seaweed, soaked by her gleeful splashing. At this spectacle, the women of the village decided that they had had enough. A group of them went to the fisherman's cottage to speak their minds. They complained about her strange ways, how her behaviour wasn't respectable and how she was setting a bad example to the other girls. The tiny fisherman's cottage seemed stuffed full of bodies and harsh voices, when suddenly they stopped and nobody moved.

Everyone was listening to the sound of the sea, or was it the sky? Wind and wave were joined in a sound no one had heard before. Immense, threatening, it seemed to make the very stones of the cottage grind together like bones.

'There will be a storm tonight. Oh! Such a storm as never was!' cried Morgan.

Then, clear above the noise of that huge sea surge came the singing. The fisherman recognised the song he had heard by the waterfall all that time ago.

'They are singing my song, they are singing my song to call me home.' Morgan wriggled through that crowded space to get to the door. The fisherman threw his arms around her for one last time, but whether it was to stop her or give her one last hug, he never knew. Her hair and clothes were already sopping wet, there was a twisting and turning like fish in a net and she was gone. That night there was such a storm as never was.

Goblin Combe

Combe is an old word for valley. The local people never went near Goblin Combe in the dark if they could help it. They knew that during the hours of darkness, the combe belonged to the goblins. The goblins weren't keen on people at all because they knew that they would steal their gold if given the chance. Gold, gem stones and other precious metals like silver come from under the earth where goblins live. That's why they believed that all treasure belongs to them.

Darkness always comes earlier in valleys and so it was dusk in the combe sooner than it ever was in the village. Local people avoided the combe from late afternoon because they knew that there could be found one of the entrances to the goblin kingdom. Or should I say exits – because at twilight the great rock that marked the threshold between our world and theirs would split open – and the goblins would come sprawling and scuttling out. They couldn't bear the sun or even the light of a dull day, but they yearned for the woods and the wider spaces.

They would follow their long pointy noses, snuffling out mushrooms to eat. In the spring and summer they would search for yellow flowers for which they had a particular liking because they reminded them of gold. However, these were hard to see in the darkness even with goblin eyes.

One spring day, a group of children went to play in the combe. They didn't need reminding to be back long before sunset. All morning they had been pestered by the youngest to be allowed to go with them. They didn't want the responsibility of looking after her, but she had worn them down with her whining. This was the first time she had been so far from the village and she was delighted with the adventure.

The day wore on and the afternoon sun slanted low through the woods around the combe. There amongst the trees she saw shining golden clumps amongst the dead leaves, and darted off alone to see what they were. Some early cowslips were blooming, with their golden flowers hanging bright against the dark earth. She picked as many as she could carry and followed the children's voices back to the path. When she reached it, everyone had gone. Somehow each child had thought that she was with another one of them. It is so easily done.

Alone in the combe, she was too young to realise the danger of the darkening day. But she was so very tired, having never been out so far and so long before. A huge rock loomed palely in the gloom. It looked like it would make a good seat to rest on. Carefully she put her bunch of cowslips on a ledge so as not to damage them when she climbed.

Suddenly the rock cracked open and a horde of goblins came pouring out of the gap. They stopped suddenly and hissed with surprise when they saw their human visitor. Fortunately for her, they also noticed the glimmering bunch of cowslips placed at their entrance. Believing that she had brought them a precious gift from her world, they excitedly seized her and dragged her down into theirs.

What a strange place it was, as she later described to the villagers. Full of mighty halls and tunnels and all lit by a soft, unearthly gleam, like starlight shimmering on water on a moonless night. The goblins showed her such wonders of treasure – heaps of gold, silver and copper and jewels the size of hen's eggs. They showed her the crowns and necklaces they had made from these for their Goblin Kings and Queens. The goblin children didn't complain about how little she was and how much trouble she would be, but played ball games with her with glowing balls made from solid gold.

At last the goblins realised that not even all these marvels could keep the child awake any longer. They carried her back along their

tunnels through the entrance to her own world. A hooting owl woke her. She was cold, soaked with dew and shivering. It was very dark. Digging hard into her back was that great rock with its clefts and lumpy ridges, but with no sign of a crack. She remembered her dream of all that lay behind it, the strange light, the treasures, the games. As she stepped away, something gleaming rolled between her legs. It was a ball made of solid gold. No dream then, but a gift to say thank you for the cowslips.

Rolling it before her along the path, she made for home. Before she left the combe she was met by an anxious search party of villagers carrying lanterns. In front was the village priest carrying a bible and some holy water, just in case.

The tale of her adventure soon spread and it reached the ears of a travelling juggler. How he would like one of those golden balls to juggle with, or, even better, to have three. How much money he could make with goblin gold flashing in the sun as he tossed and caught those balls. He asked for directions to Goblin Combe. The villagers feared for him and begged him not to go there, especially as night fell. He laughed at their warning – what was the point of going at any other time? They refused to tell him the way, but he found it anyhow.

Time had passed since the girl's adventure, but there were still some late cowslips blooming in the woods. He picked a bunch and soon found that great rock. A distant sunset faded beyond the valley, but there in the heart of the combe it was already dark. As he placed the flowers on the rock a great crack appeared and an enraged crowd of goblins burst out of it. Hissing and squeezing, they grabbed him with hard and horny hands and dragged him inside. He was never seen again.

Goblin Combe is there to this day. So is the rocky entrance to the world of the goblins. Have a care if you go there.

THE APPLE TREE MAN

Everyone knew that there was buried treasure on the farm. That old story had been turned around and around in people's mouths like the months turned the seasons and the seasons turned the years. For time beyond measure everyone knew that there was treasure, but no one could find it. The farmer spent all his time digging and looking and neglecting the farm work. He neglected his two motherless sons. Their mother had died when the younger brother was born. The older brother didn't mind because he was just like his father and all he cared about was treasure. The younger brother was different, he cared about the farm, about the animals and the crops. He kept everything going and without him there would probably have been no farm, just holes in the ground.

When the old man died, everyone was surprised to learn that he had left the farm entirely to his older son. There was nothing for the younger one, who supposed that things would carry on much as they had done before – his brother digging for treasure that wouldn't be found and him doing all the farm work. But he was in for a nasty shock. Even though it was Christmas, his brother told him to leave.

'It's all mine now and I can do what I want and I don't want you. You can move out. There's an old shed at the bottom of the orchard – you can move into that. But I'll want rent for it, you can't have it for free. I want a silver piece for that in a year's time, mind.'

The younger brother had never seen a silver piece. He had never earned any money. All his short life he had worked every day on the farm without being paid, and now in the middle of winter he was being thrown out by his own brother. Crunching across the snow to the old orchard, the tears on his cheeks were the only warmth on that short journey to another life.

The shed had half a roof and three walls. As he looked around for some timber to make repairs, two dark shapes shuffled towards him out of the gloom. Then sadness turned to anger as he saw the old ox and donkey that his brother said had been sold. Nobody had wanted to buy such old animals and the older boy had abandoned them without shelter or fodder, leaving them to starve. The younger brother scraped away snow in a nearby field and tore up grass for them. He found bark and twigs in the woods to make medicines for their sores. Under his care they began to get better. He slept between them for warmth until he had repaired the shed. He worked for neighbouring farms, earned enough to survive, earned people's good will. Neighbours gave him the bits and pieces of this and that they no longer wanted. He built a stall for the ox and donkey. Spring was coming.

With the turning of the seasons, younger brother was busier than ever. In February he pruned the neglected fruit trees. In April and May they were covered in blossom. He turned over the sweet earth and planted. By summer there were vegetables growing. The orchard was full of buzzing bees and birdsong. A stray lurcher dog came to stay, kept the rabbits off the vegetables, caught them for the pot. A stray cat came to stay, kept the rats from the stall and stores. He had made a garden out of wasteland.

Autumn came with a rich harvest. The apple trees, responding to their care after so many years, bore a huge crop. The ox and donkey grew fat on surplus apples and their owner made cider with what he couldn't give away to neighbours. At night the lurcher and the cat curled up with the ox and donkey and their snores could be heard all over the orchard, but younger brother tossed and turned on his straw mattress. He was worrying about the winter, because that was when he would have to pay the rent. There was no way he would be able to earn as much as a silver coin. Worrying doesn't keep trouble away. Winter came. Frost made the shed and stall creak, and snapped twigs from the fruit trees. The young farmer kept a careful eye on his store of wood, but for now they were cosy, the lurcher across his feet, the cat purring on his lap.

A faint tang of apple came from the dead wood he had pruned from the orchard and slowly he remembered the old custom. He remembered that winter was the time when the apple trees were thanked for their harvest. If properly thanked, they would bear good fruit the following year. Thinking that he would soon be thrown out of the orchard because he didn't have a silver piece for his brother, he decided to thank them as soon as possible. He toasted some bread and picked up a flagon of cider. He didn't have a gun to shoot between the branches to frighten bad spirits away – the lurcher's barking would have to do. Dog and man crunched across the snow to the oldest apple tree. All alone, with no family and no neighbours near, he began to sing the Wassail song. He remembered that Wassail means 'good health' in the old language, and as he wished the trees well, he threaded the toast onto the twigs and poured the cider over the trunk. As he pretended to shoot a gun through the branches, the lurcher barked furiously and across the orchard the ox bellowed and the donkey brayed.

Back at the old farmhouse his brother heard the row. He hadn't thought of the younger one for months, but surely it would soon be time for him to collect his rent. He decided to go over the next day, if only to warn him that he hadn't forgotten.

Those in the orchard turned to go back to the warmth of the fire but stopped when they heard a creaking, grating voice like the sound of branches rubbing together. The young man stared at the trunk where there was now a great mouth-like crack. Lip-like scars in the bark moved as the voice came from deep inside the tree. Bulging eyes had appeared on the lumps left by lopped branches. Bristling twigs formed eyebrows and beard. When the Apple Tree Man smiled, his bark face became covered in criss-cross wrinkles.

'Many winters since I heard that song, many winters. My thanks to you, young man, for that. I been watching you, I seen the way you been helping my people, bringing them back to health with your hard work. My thanks for that too, so I'll tell you something that will help you. Something your no-good brother is longing to know, but never will because you will get there first. You take up a spade and dig between my roots and you will see what you will see...'

The bare branches thrashed and creaked in the frost-stilled air and the old trunk shook as the Apple Tree Man laughed. Then the gnarled face faded and all was silent for a moment over the silver-white snow, until man and dog started to run. They chased each other back to the shed where the tools were, they raced each other back to the orchard where the young man began to dig in the largest hollow between the tree's old roots. The ground was hard with frost but the man was as strong as the hope that grew inside him. Before long the spade struck something that rang out with the sound of metal on metal.

Its edge had chopped clean through the ancient rotten box and chimed on the hoard of silver coins inside. The Apple Tree Man had revealed where the buried treasure had been hidden. As the man carefully carried it all back to the shed to hide it in his woodpile, it began to snow. It snowed for the rest of that night and covered up all traces of where he had been digging.

Next day he had a visitor. But not before his brother had stopped in amazement at the changes in the orchard. Now that they were so sleek and well cared for, it took him some time to recognise the ox and donkey he had left to starve. As he stared at them he too remembered an old custom, or rather something that was believed long ago. The old people used to say that so blessed were all the animals that were in the stable when baby Jesus was born that on the stroke of midnight they were given the power of human speech. Every Christmas Eve, as the clocks struck twelve, they could be heard to speak, and humans could talk to them! That gave him an idea.

He would secretly return when the time was right to ask the ox and donkey whether they knew where the treasure was hidden.

But first there was the matter of the rent. He banged on the door and was invited in.

'No need for that. I've come to tell you your rent is due. Have it ready the day after tomorrow, that will be a year to the day...' and then he left.

Christmas! Leading such a solitary life, the young farmer didn't even know that it was Christmastime. The next day he was busy. There was much to do apart from treating the animals with extra food. The short winter day was soon over and then it was Christmas Eve. Just before midnight the older brother sneaked back to the orchard and hid himself in the pile of hay in a corner of the beasts' stall. As the church clock began to strike he was about to speak to the ox when the ox spoke first:

'Are you awake, Brother Donkey?'

'Who wouldn't be with that foolish brother shuffling around in our breakfast like some giant rat?'

'Up to no good as usual. He hopes to learn the secret of the buried treasure from us. Well, we can tell him something he doesn't know…'

So eager was the hideaway to hear this news that he no longer felt the hay dust getting up his nose or the brittle stalks pricking him through his clothes.

'He'll never find that buried treasure because it is buried no longer. Buried no longer because it's been found, found and dug up. He can carry on digging and scraping until the farmhouse falls into one of his own tunnels, but he'll never find that treasure…'

The clock must have chimed the last stroke of midnight because speech gave way to a great lowing and braying which sounded like rough laughter. However harsh it sounded, it wasn't as harsh as the truth the young farmer had just heard and he sneaked back to his hollow life.

Early on Christmas morning, ox and donkey were loaded with bags and baskets. At the bottom of them was the silver, hidden by a layer of firewood. On top roosted the chickens, scolding the cat. The lurcher loped ahead whilst the younger brother led the others by their halters – off to a new life and all its adventures. When the rent collector came, he found them all gone and the shed empty but for a single silver coin gleaming on the dirt floor.

The Tree Witch

The elder tree has an extraordinary ability to grow back, no matter how many times it is cut down. If you cut off one branch, two will reappear. Maybe this is why it is believed to have magical powers. Whether it does or not, this story should have a 'Could be Scary' warning!

Of course, all trees have their special powers and uses. Some feed other creatures. Some provide medicines. Some are used for making magical spells. The elder tree, however, is the most useful for witches as they can use them as a disguise to move about in. Who would suspect that a tree would actually be a witch in disguise? That is exactly why the farmers in Somerset never used to allow an elder tree on their land, just in case.

So it was that Farmer Yeo should have known better, that night when he went out to see why his cows were so restless. He should have taken more notice of the shadow that the full moon was making behind the hedge of the cow field. A long-armed, twiggy-fingered kind of a shadow reaching over the grass to where the cows were trampling about, bunched into a corner and rolling their huge velvet eyes in fear.

The next day they gave no milk, and it was the same every day after that. Farmer Yeo knew that there was something badly wrong. He decided to wait and watch the cows secretly at night. Because he was staring at the cows until his eyes hurt in the waning moonlight, he didn't see the elder tree detach itself from the hedge. He didn't see it making its jerky way towards the animals. When he heard the creaking of its limbs, he thought it was the wind making the hedge move.

Perhaps he had dozed off for a few moments, because he suddenly saw another shape amongst the herd. It was a crouching

figure, with longer arms than could be possible and knobbly fingers that twisted beneath the cow's udders. Then he understood that an Elder Tree Witch had come to his farm. Dashing back to the farmhouse in his panic, he noticed that dawn was breaking. He knew that he would have to wait for the return of darkness before he could act.

He was in such a hurry to escape that he didn't pause to shut the gate properly – properly, that is, against witches. If he had just paused for an instant to loop the iron chain around the gate post, that might have kept her out, because creatures from the spirit world don't like to pass cold iron. If he had done that, and, just to make sure, taken a stick and drawn the shape of a cross in the ground by the gate, that would have prevented her from coming back, for sure. He had to admit that he hadn't thought of doing these things when he asked his mother to cut off one of the silver buttons she had just repaired his Sunday best jacket with. He wanted to make a silver bullet from it, because silver was another metal that would stop a witch, if it comes at them in the form of a bullet.

Farmer Yeo was brave, but foolish to think of shooting when other ways would have worked better. The next day he crept back to the cow field with his gun loaded with a silver bullet made from a crushed button. There was that fearsome shape again. This time he saw her staggering towards the cows, but he was just too late in taking his aim before she was in amongst them. Now he was worried that if he missed he might hurt one of his animals. He crept closer to make aiming easier and the Elder Tree Witch must have sensed him, the way a tree can sense us from afar. As she turned towards him, the farmer knew he had only one chance. He shot at the place where skinny branches met scraggy trunk. Buttons aren't meant to be turned into bullets – maybe it wasn't smooth enough, maybe an edge caught inside the gun barrel to make the shot go wide. Farmer Yeo missed and the witch felt the bullet whistle through her branches. Now he was the target as she lurched towards him in her rage.

For a second time he ran from that field, but if he had run fast the first time, now he ran faster than any wind. Faster than the wind he ran, but he could not escape the sound of her rage, screaming like a storm wind in her thrashing branches. His mother was waiting, but she didn't help him to close the shutters and bar the door; instead she went to put a log of ash wood on the fire. Some people believe that the ash tree also has magical powers because the first people were carved from the trunk of an ash tree. They believe that an ash tree will always help people if it can.

Everyone in the farmhouse could hear the Elder Tree Witch tearing at the shutters and battering the doors. With each scream they could hear strips of wood being torn away. It would only be a matter of time before she was inside the house. Mother Yeo went to the burning ash log and heaped it onto a spade. She made her terrified son open the door just as the witch hurled herself at it. Just in time, Mother Yeo flung the burning log at the witch where her branches joined her trunk.

There was a scream that tore the air apart as the elder tree burst into flames – a tower of flame, a fountain of sparks, and then nothing but a heap of ashes on the ground.

'No more trouble from she,' said Mother Yeo, who went to fetch the iron poker. She prodded through the ashes until they were a nice smooth mound, and then with the tip of the poker she drew the shape of a cross on the top.

'No more trouble from she, not now nor evermore,' she said.

When news of the story got out, the neighbours went to see whether anything had happened to any of the women they suspected of being a witch. Two were at home as usual and as for Raggy Liddy, well she was never seen again. The only sign that she had ever lived in that cottage was a large heap of warm ashes in the fireplace.

PART TWO

PEOPLE WE SHOULD KNOW ABOUT

A Prince Amongst the Pigs

There was once a prince called Bladud who was the King and Queen's only child. How proud they were of him until the day he showed them something shameful. He had returned from his travels with a terrible disease called leprosy. It was now eating away at his skin, which was covered in pale blotches like a fungus. In those days there was no cure. People who had leprosy were called lepers and had to live far away from everyone else to stop them passing on the illness. They were forced to live alone or in groups of other lepers. If they went anywhere they had to ring a bell to warn healthy people to keep their distance. Now the prince, heir to the throne, would have to leave the palace and everything he had known.

Before he left, the Queen gave him her ruby ring so that he would always remember who he was and where he came from, even if he was never allowed to return. What a cruel gift that was! Prince Bladud hid the ring in his robes and left the palace. Soon all his money was spent and he didn't know what to do to survive. He joined a group of lepers who had become beggars. By now his royal robes had become rags. When the other lepers asked where he came from and he tried to tell them the truth, they just looked at his rags and laughed. Soon he was too ashamed to say that he was a prince and before long he left them and tried to find work.

At last he came to a distant farm. The farmer took pity on him and said that he needed a swineherd (who is someone who looks after pigs). In those days, pigs would roam the forest and the swineherds would look after them, making sure that they didn't get lost or eaten by wolves. This meant that Bladud could live alone in the wilds but the farmer would pay him enough to survive, so Bladud was grateful.

Spring was turning into summer and Bladud found peace in the leafy beauty of the forest. Although he was sometimes lonely, missing his parents and his friends at the palace, at least here under the spreading green of the trees he didn't have to hide from people or lie about who he was. Summer had slipped into autumn and Bladud knew that when the pigs had grown fat on the fallen acorns, he would have to take them back to the farm. Then, to his horror, he noticed that their skin was showing the signs of his disease. The pigs had caught his leprosy!

Fearing the farmer's anger, he drove the pigs deeper into the forest. He didn't know how he would survive the winter and he didn't know how he could risk returning to the farm with a whole herd of diseased pigs. In his despair, he let the pigs wander where they wanted. Instead of herding he was following them.

They reached a place in the forest where even from a distance Bladud could see a mist amongst the branches. There was also a peculiar smell that he couldn't explain and which was quite strange to him. He could hear popping and gurgling noises but couldn't understand where they were coming from. As he drew closer he noticed that the air was much warmer and that the leaves were still green instead of the yellows and browns of autumn. Then the pigs rushed towards a hollow and started wallowing and rolling, squealing with delight. Bladud followed them and saw that they had thrown themselves into a pool of mud that was oozing and spurting out of the ground. This was the source of the strange smell and the mud itself was warm – as warm as the baths he had enjoyed as a prince. Then he understood that the mist amongst the trees was steam and the leaves were still green because in this forest glade it was as warm as summer.

The pigs rolled in the mud for days, only emerging for long enough to stuff themselves with acorns. Eventually they seemed to lose interest, and allowed Bladud to brush the dried mud off them with handfuls of twigs. To his astonishment, all the signs of leprosy had disappeared! What if this strange smelling mud, bubbling from the ground, had some magical ingredient that cured the disease? Prince Bladud had nothing to lose and there was nobody to see him if he wallowed in the mud like the pigs. What fun it was to roll around in that warm, squelchy mess! In a few days, he too was cured of leprosy.

Bladud returned the pigs to the farmer and then he went back to the palace. He no longer had a disease but he had been living in the forest for months and the guards refused to let this filthy wild man in. The Prince knew that if he tried to tell them who he really was, he would be locked up as a madman. Then he recognised one of them, whom he had known since boyhood. A good, honest man, someone you could trust. How old he seemed now, but still with the same steady gaze, the same quiet manner. From a pocket amongst his layers of rags, he took the ruby ring that his mother had given him such a long time ago. Prince Bladud gave it to this guard, asking him to put it into the Queen's wine without her noticing. The guard took the ring and silently turned it over and over in his rough hand. Then he gave the Prince a long, deep look and, still without saying anything, went and did what he was asked.

At first the Queen didn't notice the wine-red ruby in her drink. When there was less wine and she had to tilt her cup more, something hard bobbed against her lip. She remembered the ring immediately and asked how it came to be there, but when her son was brought into the great hall she didn't recognise him until his filthy beard and hair had been cut.

How happy were parents and child now that the family had been reunited. How happy were the courtiers to reclaim their Prince. How happy were the poor and sick people of that place now that a cure for leprosy and other illnesses had been found.

As soon as power had been restored to him, the grateful prince gave the farmer a large piece of land. He also bought all the farmer's pigs and allowed them to die of old age instead of turning them into sausages. Those healing muddy springs were turned into medicinal baths where people came from all over to find cures. They gave our beautiful city of Bath its name. The mud was turned into all kinds of medicinal potions and ointments and sold far away. The prince, who was by now King Bladud, was always grateful to those pigs and called it his 'Magic Oinkment'. He used to say that if he rubbed it on his body in a special way, it would even help him to fly, and nobody quite knew whether he was joking or not!

THE HOLY THORN TREE

A thousand or so years ago, the huge Roman Empire stretched from the Middle East all the way to Wales, where it stopped at the Atlantic Ocean. As there were no cars or planes in those days, it was an enormous area to conquer and rule.

One of the reasons Britain was so important to the Romans was because, deep in the ground, there lay a rare and precious metal. This wasn't gold or silver, it was tin. Tin was so important because it was needed for making bronze, another metal that had been used for thousands of years. That was such a long and important time that we call it the

Bronze Age. Weapons, cutlery, pots, beakers, money and even jewellery were made out of bronze. That is why tin was so precious and that was why you had to have a special licence to mine and sell it.

Someone who had a licence was a tin merchant called Joseph of Arimathea. He came all the way from the other edge of the Roman Empire, from a land which he called Israel, but which the Romans had renamed Palestine when they conquered it. Joseph was a rich and powerful man to be able to travel those distances and survive all the dangers of storms and pirates. He also had powerful friends in Somerset, including the chief of the local tribe. Joseph paid miners in Cornwall to dig tunnels deep underground and hack out the rock where tin could be found. Because they didn't have lorries or trains in those days, the tin was carried in boats. These came right into Somerset where there was a port near Glastonbury. Through his tin trading, he brought wealth to the area as well as many stories about the marvels to be found in all the lands he travelled through.

This Joseph was also Jesus' uncle, or to be exact, his great uncle. Back home, Jesus was causing trouble by trying to start a new religion. This made the Romans suspicious of him. Some of the local people were suspicious too, but some of them agreed with Jesus and wanted to follow his teachings. Jesus spoke out against what he thought was wrong. He spoke up for what he thought was right. More and more people agreed with him and followed him about the country to listen and came to believe in what he was saying. That made the Romans very angry, and he was put into prison and then killed. His uncle begged for his body and buried it. He knew that because he loved Jesus, believed in his teachings and was a family member, his life would also be in danger. He knew that he should get as far away from Roman Palestine as possible.

He made his way back to Somerset by boat, as he had done so many times before. This time he knew that it would never be safe to return. Perhaps we can now think of Jesus' uncle as our most famous refugee. He arrived at what we now call Wearyall Hill, which used to be the

shore of the lake that surrounded Glastonbury. You can still clearly see where the water used to come up to. In his hand he held a wooden staff, like a large walking stick. Some say that it was cut from the wooden cross where Jesus died. The slope was steep and Joseph leaned on this piece of wood to help him climb it. As soon as the staff touched the ground, the dead wood burst into blossom and leaves.

'This is a good and holy land,' said Joseph when he saw what had happened. He planted the staff in the ground, where it took root and grew into a tree which blossomed twice a year – at Easter and at Christmas, the most important Christian festivals.

Then the local chieftain gave Joseph, and the friends who had travelled with him, twelve pieces of land that were never known to flood. The Romans had killed Jesus, but they couldn't kill his ideas. On one of these pieces of land Joseph built the first Christian church to be found anywhere outside Palestine. In time, this became Glastonbury Abbey, which was once the greatest in Britain.

THE MAGIC
CANNONBALL

Elizabeth Sydenham was more than beautiful and extremely rich. She could have married any man she chose in the whole country, but she only wanted to marry Francis Drake and her father wouldn't allow it. Francis was only a farmer's son, whereas Elizabeth was born to one of the most important families in Somerset. That could have been reason enough, but some people say there was another. Francis was said to be a magician, and in those days you could be burned to death as a punishment for practising magic.

People were just beginning to get used to the idea that the world was round, not flat. Very few believed that it was shaped like a ball and even today we still refer to 'the four corners of the Earth'. Francis, however, did believe that the world was globe-shaped and became the first Englishman to sail around it. Many said that he only managed it because of his magical powers, but none dared to say it in public. You might think that being the eldest of twelve brothers (and we don't know how many sisters) would have been enough to drive him as far away from home as possible. In any case, the Queen was very pleased with him because he was the best explorer, so she knighted him. Being such a good sailor and fighter, he became a successful treasure-seeker, stealing gold from the Spanish at sea and on land.

Now that he was 'Sir' Francis Drake, rich, famous and a national hero, you would imagine that Elizabeth's father would no longer object to the marriage. But he still did, probably because of that awkward story about Francis being a magician. Elizabeth was still forbidden to marry him. And where was he anyway? Francis hadn't been seen for years – he was off on one of his treasure-hunting explorations again. After all, it had taken him three years to sail round the world; maybe he would never come back – which is what George Sydenham said and secretly prayed for.

Finally, Elizabeth was persuaded to marry someone else. Maybe she believed that Francis had been lost at sea or maybe she hoped he would rescue her at the last minute. As she stood at the altar with her fiancé in Monksilver's church, there was a huge crash.

The door didn't even have time to burst open as a cannonball smashed right through it and rolled up the aisle towards the couple. They sprang apart just in time as it crashed and ground its way to where they had been standing. Everyone knew that it had been sent by Sir Francis Drake himself from wherever he was in the world to prevent the marriage. There was no arguing with the power of that kind of magic and the wedding was cancelled.

Next day, Sir Francis' boat arrived at Plymouth and Elizabeth was allowed to marry him at last, probably because her father

was too frightened to stand up to Francis and his special talents. Elizabeth insisted on keeping the cannonball at her father's home, Combe Sydenham, as a souvenir. You can see it there to this day. We now know that it is a meteorite, a lump of mineral that fell to Earth from outer space. Well, that just shows how strong Sir Francis' magic was to be able to conjure such an object from the sky!

To the Spanish he was a pirate and to the English he was a hero. That is why he commanded the English warships, fighting the Spanish when they sailed to England to get their revenge. When the enemy fleet was sighted, he wouldn't stop playing his game of bowls, rolling them here and there like firing cannonballs slowly. You would think that he would be more interested in the approaching war than in playing. However, people knew that he was using them for his magic, casting 'spells of divination', which is how magicians see into the future. We still marvel at how so many of the Spanish ships were set on fire, but shouldn't be so surprised given that the name 'Drake' is an old word for dragon.

As for Elizabeth's father, he was still bitter about her marriage. They say he never got over it and his unhappy life gave him an unquiet death – which is why he still haunts the road near Combe Sydenham. He can be seen, a headless ghost riding up and down on a ghostly horse, carrying his head under his arm. Some say that if he comes across Drake he will hurl it at him like a cannonball.

BEST KING, WORST COOK

We can't all be good at everything, but Alfred very nearly was. To begin with he was a great scholar, which means he was good at learning. Although he was the youngest of four brothers, he beat them all when his mother set them a test. This was to learn a whole book of poems. In those days, books were as valuable as jewels because they all had to be written and decorated by hand. Alfred learned all the poems by heart and won the book.

Many of you who don't like poetry will be thinking, 'So what?'

But this skill was later to help Alfred win the war against the Danes.

He became a great soldier, and was crowned king after his brothers died in battle. He grew up in troubled times, with Danish invaders taking more and more land and selling the local people into slavery. British chiefs and kings were also fighting each other. Sometimes they even joined forces with their Danish enemies to gang up on their own countrymen. In fact, there wasn't really a country at all – just kingdoms where the borders changed after each battle, and there were plenty of those.

Alfred was determined to stop the Danes from taking any more land. He even gave some of them 'tribute' – paying them treasure to stay where they were. Nobody trusted anyone else and any agreements didn't last for long. Then Alfred lost an important battle and needed to go into hiding.

In those days the Somerset Levels were a maze of swamps and waterways. Only the local people knew the secret tracks across the peat-dark waters. Following these, they could reach lumps of firm ground, small islands where the reeds grew tall enough to hide most things. The tracks were made from narrow logs tied together, and were a way of getting around without using boats. Local people had been using them for thousands of years. They knew how to raise them so that people could walk safely across. They also knew how to hide them by lowering them beneath the surface of the water. There they were so well hidden that an enemy could be standing right next to one and not notice. Along these paths came other fugitives – people who needed to run away from trouble, just like Alfred. Most of these were soldiers who wanted another chance to fight the Danes. If enough of them could regroup they might win next time.

King Alfred reached this refuge in disguise. He thought it would be much safer if nobody recognised him. There was a price on his head, which meant that the Danes would pay a reward to anyone who told them where the king was. A kind woman let him stay in her little house. If she wondered what was in that sack he was carrying, she didn't ask. When times are dangerous it can be better not to ask too many questions.

In the sack was Alfred's harp. Disguised as a poor travelling musician, he was welcome everywhere. He was even welcomed in the Danish warriors' camps. Now you will realise how useful learning poetry can be. In those days, stories were made into long poems and sung. Alfred was a brilliant entertainer. When he sang, everyone fell silent. When he took a break, his listeners started to talk. In the Danish camps they talked about war plans and Alfred, pretending to tune his harp strings, did the listening. He had become a spy, spying for himself.

One day he was in the kind woman's house, brooding about what he had heard. He was wondering how he could use this secret knowledge to make his own plans. The woman explained that she had to go out and asked her guest to watch the cakes and make sure that they didn't burn. Alfred nodded, but he wasn't really listening. He didn't want to be distracted from a plan that was forming. She was too busy to notice his lack of attention and hurried off. She wasn't gone long, but when she came back, it was just in time to see the cakes burning black. Alfred was still staring into space and she was furious.

'I have given you food and shelter and you can't even do the simplest thing for me in return!' Then she punched him, hard, in the arm.

Alfred had been shocked out of his daydream. It took him a few moments to guess what must have happened. He felt terribly sorry, knowing how difficult it is to find food in war time. He apologised and explained that because he was king, he had so many worries and so many plans to make. He had been concentrating so hard on planning his next battle against the Danes that he hadn't noticed the terrible burning smell.

Then it was her turn to be shocked. This raggedy man was her king and she had punched him! It was also her turn to apologise.

Maybe she had something to do with it – maybe she knew the right people to talk to, the right people to send messages by in those troubled times – but suddenly more and more warriors came to join Alfred. He now had a secret army which was not to stay secret for long. King Alfred fought the Danish warlord one more time, for the last time, because Alfred won. He then made peace with his conquered enemy, and was able to create a new kingdom called Wessex. Now that there was peace in Wessex, other parts of the land followed that example and that was the beginning of England becoming a country.

To say thank you, Alfred built a special church in the place that had hidden him. He wanted to give people the chance to live in peace and create beautiful things like the book of poems he had won as a child. He was so good at everything (except cooking!) – performing, fighting, making friends, learning and building. He was called 'Alfred the Great', the only English king to be given that title.

When I was out walking near where this happened, I was shown some curious black lumps growing on sticks and logs. They are

a kind of fungus, like a mushroom (only don't try to eat them). They are called 'King Alfred's Cakes' because they look just like burnt muffins or buns. Curiously they are what country people used for lighting fires, the old-fashioned way, from sparks.

A Headless Saint (But Not for Long!)

The people who lived on the coast were used to seeing boats criss-crossing the mighty River Severn as it widened into the sea. On that day they were amazed to see a stranger approaching on an even stranger vessel. This wasn't a boat, as such, just his old cloak spread out on the water – but behaving just like a boat. Not only did the cloak carry the holy man Decuman, but also a large cow. By the time this extraordinary sight had approached the shore, a crowd had gathered to see them land.

Everyone watched as the two of them climbed the hill beyond the port. Decuman and his cow settled near a lovely spring of fresh water. This pure spring had never run dry and had been a special and holy place ever since people had first lived in the area. There Decuman spent his time praying, milking his cow and trying to tell everyone about the new Christian religion. Despite seeing his marvellous arrival, nobody wanted to listen. One day when he was milking, somebody crept up behind him. To this day no one can agree whether it was a local person or a marauding Danish pirate, but this somebody silently took the axe from his belt. He chopped off Decuman's head, which bounced and rolled to the bottom of the hill.

Decuman stood up and followed his head downhill. He picked it up and replaced it on his neck where it stuck back on as though nothing had happened. Then he climbed back up the hill, looking just the same, and finished milking his cow.

His executioner, the man who had chopped off his head, watched all of this in astonished silence. He could only believe his eyes when he saw Decuman drinking the milk with none of it leaking from where his head joined his neck. People say that after witnessing this miracle, the executioner was the first to be baptised in the holy well.

Many soon followed, and when Decuman died he became a saint. Today you can see the church that was built later and named Saint Decuman's. The spring is still there, as clear and fresh as ever. Its water tastes as sweet as the golden plums you can pick from the branches hanging over it.

KING ARTHUR AND EXCALIBUR

King Arthur had a magical sword called Excalibur. Some say that he was the only one who could pull the sword from the stone into which it had been wedged. When he and no one else was able to do this, it proved that Arthur was the true king of all the Britons. Some say that Excalibur was given to him later, when he had already proved himself to be a good and just king. In this version, the sword was given to him by a magical being, the Lady of the Lake. Many believe that this happened in the lake that surrounded Glastonbury Tor.

In King Arthur's time, the area around Glastonbury Tor was covered by a vast expanse of water. Whole rivers disappeared into it. Water-smoothed islands showed less or more of their round green backs as the waters rose and fell with the seasons. Long ago that vast lake was drained. Now flat green land spreads around the Tor instead of water. You can clearly see the five rivers that coil their way across like great silver dragons on their way to the sea. Towns and villages have since grown across the backs of those islands but the local people know that from time to time the flat land can quickly disappear beneath the floodwaters again.

On the way to Glastonbury there is an ancient bridge called Pomparle's Bridge. That isn't the name of a person, it is an old word that used to mean 'the dangerous bridge'. It was dangerous because of the floodwaters that swirled around it. It was dangerous because Arthur's best knights would take it in turns to stand on it, guarding the only way you could get to Glastonbury by dry land.

One day, King Arthur was in a hurry, galloping along and not even slowing down to get across the bridge. But he had to rein in his horse very suddenly because there in front of him, blocking his way, was an enormous knight. You know what it can be like when you are in a rush and people get in your way. Sometimes temper happens before thought. He didn't recognise this stranger, but the stranger should have recognised him.

'Make way for your king! Stand aside at once!' Arthur shouted.

The huge man and his horse did not move.

'I warned you, you fool. How dare you disobey the King of all the Britons!' and Arthur drew his sword, which meant that he was going to lose no time in fighting his way across.

As the stranger's sword left its scabbard, its answering hiss of steel echoed Excalibur's menace. The horses neighed and screamed and tried to jostle each other off the bridge and the men hacked and thrust with their weapons.

In those days, knights were allowed to fight any other knight as long as they were fully armed. It was often a way of settling arguments or it was done as a kind of sport. This time it certainly wasn't a game. Arthur fought on, confident that with Excalibur he would win – even though his opponent was bigger, stronger, faster and better trained. Then as the fighting sapped his anger he had to admit that he wasn't winning: he was slowly but surely being pushed back along the bridge. He also realised that this glorious fighter could already have unhorsed or even killed him several times, but had chosen not to. At that realisation he felt a surge of bitter pride as hasty and hot as his anger had been. He called upon the Lady of the Lake: 'You promised me that Excalibur was a magical sword and could not be defeated in battle!'

He thrust again at his enemy and Excalibur shattered. The other knight immediately sheathed his own sword to show that he would not fight an unarmed man. He towered over Arthur, who by now was kneeling on the bridge, gathering up the broken pieces in a daze. He stumbled to his feet, cradling the glinting shards in his arms, when all around the two men there came a swell of sound.

The reeds whispered, the water murmured and the willow leaves shivered and amongst them could be heard the voice of a woman.

'I promised that Excalibur could not be defeated in battle. This was no battle. It was a quarrel brought on by haste and anger and pride. It was not worthy of the King of all the Britons. It was not worthy of Excalibur.'

Arthur knew that the Lady of the Lake was right. He tipped the broken pieces over the edge of the bridge and watched the water swallow them. Moments later the skin of the water parted as a woman's arm appeared. The sleeve shone silvery white; droplets bright as crystals poured down it. But far brighter than all of these was what she held in her hand. It was Excalibur. Excalibur healed, mended and made new. Kneeling, King Arthur took it once more from the Lady of the Lake.

He turned to the knight who had defeated him and met Sir Lancelot for the first time.

Sir Lancelot who had just arrived all the way from France and who had never before seen the King of all the Britons and could not therefore have recognised him. Sir Lancelot who was to become the bravest knight of all the Knights of the Round Table and who was never defeated in combat.

After that adventure, it was said that the blade of Excalibur had become so bright that sometimes it was enough just to unsheathe it to prevent trouble. Held high, its light could be seen for miles. The sight of that brilliance was enough to send Arthur's enemies running without any need to strike a blow.

Time passed and King Arthur and his knights had many magical and brave adventures. Some say that he was the best king Britain ever had. Even so, no hero lasts forever and after Britain's Golden Age, Arthur fought and lost his last battle. How all of that happened is another story.

During that battle Arthur was wounded so badly that he knew he would soon die. Many of his friends had been killed and so it was that he found himself with only one companion, the faithful knight Sir Bedivere.

At first Bedivere could not bring himself to believe that the battle was lost or that his king was going to die. Arthur had difficulty in persuading him, but most of all he worried about Excalibur getting into the wrong hands. Too badly hurt to do it himself, he begged Bedivere to take the sword to Pomparle's Bridge and throw it into the water. Bedivere promised to do this, but when he reached those swirling waters, he couldn't bear to get rid of such a precious weapon. He decided to hide it and come back for it later – especially as he still half hoped that Arthur would recover. Wouldn't he be glad of it then? So Bedivere hid it in a hollow willow tree instead, and hurried back to his friend.

'Did you throw Excalibur into the flood?' asked the king, his voice much weaker by now.

'Yes, my king.'

'And what did you see?'

'I saw mist over the water.'

'You are lying to me. Now go and do as I ask. Do what your king commands you before it is too late.'

Bedivere went back to the bridge, confused. How did Arthur know that he hadn't thrown the sword in the water? He took Excalibur from the hollow willow. He tried to make himself throw it, but then he had another thought. Now he really did believe that Arthur was dying, his voice had sounded so feeble. All the more need, then, for a magical weapon. Bedivere was still alive, should he not keep the sword to use it himself? Again he put it back inside the tree and returned to Arthur.

'Did you throw Excalibur into the water?' His voice was now hard to hear.

'Yes, my king.'

'And what did you see?'

'I saw the sun setting over the water.'

'Again you have lied to me. The sun will never rise again over the land where there is not one man I can trust. I have asked you and I have commanded you. Now I beg you to throw Excalibur into the water.'

Bedivere hurried back to the bridge. He seized the sword and dragged it out of its scabbard. The blade blazed so brightly he almost needed to close his eyes. Squinting, he threw it over the side. Even with his eyes screwed up, he could not deny what happened next. He ran back to the king, reaching him just in time. His voice was now only a whisper.

'Did you throw Excalibur over the bridge?'

'Yes, my king.'

'And what did you see?'

'I saw a woman's arm rise from the water, bright as the sword itself. I saw the sword slowly falling towards her open hand. I saw her hand grasp the hilt and hold Excalibur high for a moment. For that moment the waters stopped rushing, the wind stopped racing and all was stillness and light. Then the arm sank back into the depth until even the point of the sword could be seen no more. Then wind and water were astir again in the dark.'

Too weak now even to whisper, Arthur smiled. Bedivere held his hand until Arthur's slipped from his grasp.

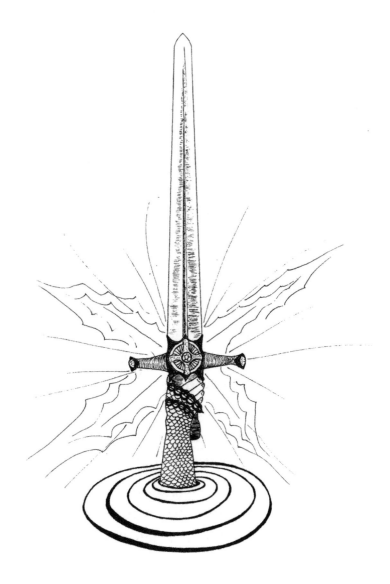

Arthur was such a great king that even after his death many could not believe that he was gone forever. There had been so many magical deeds when he had been alive, why couldn't that same magic bring him back?

And so the legends started: he was asleep with his knights under Cadbury Castle near where his last battle was fought; you could drink from the well there on Midsummer's Eve and in your dreams that night you would see him asleep and, still asleep, he would answer any question you asked. Every seven years, during a June full moon, he would ride with his knights from Camelot to Glastonbury – hadn't they found a silver horseshoe which is now in the museum? When Britain faced its greatest danger, surely he would return to stand against it?

There is a story that King Arthur comes back to Glastonbury Tor every year to stop a fight that would otherwise go on forever. A very powerful friend of his once helped him to hunt a monstrous wild pig, kill a giant and defeat a vicious witch who lived in a cave. That was in the days when people believed that some men and women were related to the many gods that were worshipped on this island before Christianity came with its one God.

Arthur's companion on these adventures, Gwyn ap Nudd (pronounced Gwin ap Neath) was one of these; more than a man and less than a god – a divine hero. Another such warrior, Gwythyr, wanted to marry Gwyn's sister. Gwyn was not going to let that happen. He thought that Gwythyr was not good enough for her, because he was just a man and not descended from a god. He took his sister and hid her away under Glastonbury Tor. Gwythyr came to rescue her. Gwyn fought to keep him away, and Gwythyr fought back. Gwyn might have been half god, but Gwythyr was desperate and would have fought to the death for the woman he loved. Neither of them could win, neither could lose and neither was going to give up.

Torn between them was the woman, whose name in the language of that time meant 'heart'. Being Gwyn's sister, she too was descended from a god and was

worshipped as a goddess of the land. How her heart must have hurt seeing the two men she loved fighting over her. At last the noise of their conflict on Glastonbury Tor disturbed Arthur, even though he was sleeping his death sleep with his knights under Cadbury Castle. Still sleeping, he seized Excalibur and made his way to the Tor. One sweep of his sword parted the fighters. He pronounced judgement: every May Eve, they would be allowed to fight from dusk to dawn. When the sun rose on May Day, the goddess would live above ground with her lover for six months. As she is a goddess of the land, that is when we have spring and summer. When October ends and we have our Halloween festival celebrating the growing dark, she goes to stay with her brother underground beneath the Tor. Then she pulls the flowers back into the earth. She calls the leaves from the trees, and spreads them over the ground to keep them nearer to her. We call that time autumn and winter.

PART THREE

HOW THINGS HAPPENED

How Hedgehog Became Spiky

Maybe you already know that animals didn't appear on Earth all at once. Somerset has its own story about how they were created and it couldn't have happened without all that lovely mud produced by the five rivers that meander across the Somerset Levels and drain into the Bristol Channel.

They say that the Great Creator often used to visit here, Somerset being his or her favourite county. Sometimes the Creator (God for short) would take on a shape that included fingers and toes, just to squish around in the mud, feeling that delicious smooth slippery substance oozing under their feet and through their hands. Don't most of us enjoy doing that if we get the chance?

One day it occurred to God that although the woods and hills and rivers were extra beautiful, it was all rather quiet. Some more sound and movement was needed and that meant creating animals. Being by the River Parrett and it being low tide at the time, divine toes stirred up the mud and divine fingers squeezed out the extra water and began to pat, pinch and prod this muddy clay into the shape of animals. The clay figures were put on the river bank and when they were dry enough not to fall apart but still wet enough to be able to move, God breathed on them to give them life. All those animals then rushed off to where they would live – whether it was woods, meadows, rivers or sea. They wriggled, bounded, flew, scuttled and swam. Somerset was full of movement, as well as all the wonderful sounds of birdsong, grunting, splashing, crashing and digging.

The work took all day, and just as your mother sometimes says that she only has one pair of hands, so did God, just then, who was therefore only making one animal at a time. This meant that one of them had to be last, and it just so happened to be Hedgehog. There he was, with his little ears perfectly shaped already hearing all the other animals having fun around him. Although his little pointy nose could smell delicious worms and slugs, he wasn't quite finished because he hadn't been given any covering except for his skin. Then, as the evening air cooled and the mists rose from the river, God sneezed, accidentally breathing life into Hedgehog before he was completely finished.

Hedgehog was in a hurry to join in with the fun that all the other animals were having, and scuttled off into the bushes before he had any proper covering on his skin. No fur, no feathers, no scales, just bare skin that shivered in the winter, burned in the summer, and was stung by insects and nettles. Because he was uncomfortable all the time he was always complaining, and this made all the other animals cross with him. You might know what it is like to live near someone who is always moaning and groaning – it's no fun at all.

The next time God visited his favourite county, there was an angry crowd of creatures complaining about Hedgehog and demanding that God do something about him. To make everyone happy, God decided to allow Hedgehog to choose any covering of any animal he could think of, and Hedgehog couldn't wait to get started.

He rushed off into the woods and came across Bear, envying his luxurious thick coat.

'Just right for winter,' thought Hedgehog. 'But wait a minute, too hot and heavy for summer.'

There was Deer chewing tree bark.

'Perfect! Cool enough for summer and warm enough for winter. Shame about the colour – rather a dull brown. I'm sure I could do better than that.'

Hedgehog was trotting across a fallen branch that bridged a shallow stream. Beneath him darted tiny silver fish. He clasped his little paws together and squeaked.

'Beautiful! I could be covered with shimmering, shining, silver fish scales!'

And he did a little dance on the branch.

'But don't fish get rather smelly when they dry out? No, that would never do.'

And on he went. Then Robin flew past him.

'That's it, feathers!' cried Hedgehog. 'Warm and fluffy in winter and cool and light in summer. What lovely red feathers Robin has, I could be covered in them.'

Then Hedgehog had a thought that made him stop where he was, even though a bramble was sticking into him on one side and a nettle brushing him on the other. He remembered that God had said: 'Any covering from any animal…'

'That means that I can have any covering from any bird I choose! I want blue feathers from Blue Tit, black from Blackbird, green from Woodpecker, white from Barn Owl, turquoise and orange from Kingfisher, yellow from Goldfinch…' and the list went on.

When he had finished he found himself covered in a glorious colourful ball of glossy feathers. God had kept his promise and not only was Hedgehog the most comfortable creature, he was also the most beautiful.

At first the other animals didn't recognise him, but when they did they gasped in wonder. Some of them even bowed low because he was so magnificent. Instead of being avoided, Hedgehog was now the centre of attention and he couldn't get enough of it. The more he was admired, the prouder he became. He strutted about with his little pointy nose in the air, which became more turned up and pointy by the day. He was too proud to share the woodland paths with other animals and made them step aside with impatient gestures of his little paws. He ordered the birds to bring him worms and the squirrels to make him nests of dry leaves. If he had been difficult to live with before, he was far worse now.

Next time God visited his favourite county he was met by an even angrier crowd of animals still complaining about Hedgehog.

'Leave it to me,' said God, and it didn't take him long to know what to do.

It was autumn and Hedgehog was getting ready for his long winter sleep. This meant that he was ordering the squirrels to bring him piles of leaves of exactly the right softness, size and colour. He gruntled himself into their welcoming layers, fell asleep and started to have a bad dream. Well, you know what it is like to have a bad dream, the best way of making it better is to wake up – then you know it was only a dream. Imagine what it must be like to have a bad dream for as long as it takes spring to arrive, which is when hedgehogs wake up. Hedgehog was dreaming that he was being turned inside out, just as we have seen our parents turning a duvet cover inside out. It was the most peculiar and uncomfortable feeling.

At last spring came and Hedgehog woke up, very hungry for breakfast as he hadn't eaten for months. He trotted along the woodland paths, too hungry to notice the astonished looks from the other animals. There was a large puddle in front of him and he had to slow down to go round it. He was surprised that the weird looking animal beside him didn't step aside. In fact, as he approached, it drew nearer. Hedgehog had grown used to everyone giving way to him, and he wasn't going to back down. He gave the stranger an extra hard look and the stranger returned it. Hedgehog drew closer and closer to that bright stare, that ridiculous upturned pointy nose and those strange spiky shafts that this animal was covered with. He drew so close that his ridiculous upturned pointy nose touched the surface of the puddle and the stranger disappeared.

Hedgehog realised that he had been looking at his own reflection all along. He also realised that his bad dream had come true and he really had been turned inside out. Those beautiful colourful feathers were now on the inside and it was their hard quills which were now on the outside.

If you come across Hedgehog today he is still making grumpy grunting noises, complaining about the beautiful colours he lost. He also scuttles extra fast because those fluffy feathers inside are tickling him wherever he goes.

The First Christmas Pudding

King Arthur's father once had a best friend who was the kindest, most generous man in all the land. His name was Sir Cleges (pronounced Sir Cleggies!) and tales of his present-giving had spread far and wide. When the old king died, Sir Cleges went to live near Camelot where Arthur ruled. There he was welcomed and soon became a favourite with everyone because of his generosity. He learned the ways of the court and praised Arthur's custom of never starting the evening meal until they had been told about some new marvel or wonder. Sir Cleges also enjoyed being as generous as ever in his own home. His favourite hobby was to give lavish parties and to make sure that every guest went home with an expensive present. Some people say that he invented party bags!

Much as she loved and admired her husband, Lady Cleges was getting worried. She knew that her husband was giving away more than they could afford. Not enough money was coming into their home to pay for this overgenerous lifestyle. Soon there was not enough to pay the servants and they left to find work elsewhere. They spread the story of how Sir Cleges was becoming poorer and poorer. King Arthur heard about this and wondered how he could help his father's old friend, knowing that he would be too proud to accept a gift or loan of money. Despite his wife's warnings, parties were still given and guests still came, even though they had heard how poor their host had become.

At last there was not enough left to feed his own family – never mind anyone else. With no wages and no food in the house, even their beloved cook had left them. Sir

Cleges realised how foolish he had been and wondered how he would overcome his pride and beg for help. He laid his head on the stone windowsill and thought how cold and hard their lives would become. He tearfully prayed for an answer. When he had finished praying he couldn't bear to see how empty and grim his house had become since his wife had sold all their beautiful furniture and tapestries for food. So he looked out of the window instead, and saw a strange sight.

Hardly able to believe his eyes he called for Lady Cleges. Together they stared at their ancient cherry tree with its bare winter branches. As they watched, even though it was the month of December, they saw the tree become covered with foaming white cherry blossom. The scent of those flowers filled their home. Then they saw the petals blow away as each twig burst into leaf and tiny round green fruits appeared. Within moments they had swelled and ripened into deep red juicy cherries. They rushed into the courtyard where Sir Cleges took off his coat and lifted his wife into the tree. How she laughed as she tucked up her long skirts and scrambled amongst the branches. Quickly she started to pick the cherries and threw them down onto the coat. She hadn't had so much fun since she had been a girl, climbing trees in her father's orchards. When every cherry had been gathered, a pile of crimson fruit glowed beneath the bare branches.

They hurried inside with the fruit. But when they retrieved it from the bundled coat they were dismayed. It seemed as though the seasons had continued to rush along, and now the summer ripening of the cherries had been overtaken by autumn. There the cherries lay on the kitchen table, withered and dried like the last autumn leaves. Then Sir Cleges remembered that when he had been rich, he had been able to buy dried fruit from distant lands. In those days, raisins, sultanas and apricots were terribly expensive. Because they came from hot countries far away they had a long journey by donkeys, carts and boats. If they were dried they survived the journey. Most people couldn't afford them and if they could, they were considered a great luxury.

Sir Cleges rushed around the kitchen looking into the darkest corners of the cupboards and on the highest of the shelves. Soon he had a miserable collection of odds and ends on the table: a heap of stale breadcrumbs, a few forgotten pinches of spices wrapped in leaves, the scrapings of hardened honey in a jar, a handful of withered apples, some smears of butter, forgotten dregs of wine and brandy. He put all of these into a bowl with the cherries and mixed everything up with some water. Then he covered the bowl and placed it in a pan of water on the fire and set it to boil. Soon the kitchen was full of the most delicious smells. The miracle was continuing. Sir Cleges had created the most delicious pudding and Lady Cleges, her mouth watering, couldn't wait to eat it. She was so disappointed when her husband would not let her.

'Don't you see what we must do?' he cried. 'We must take it to Camelot and give it to King Arthur as a gift.'

'Would you give away our last morsel of food when we are about to starve in the midst of winter?' she replied.

'But this is no ordinary food. Remember how King Arthur refuses to allow the evening banquet to begin before someone has told of a miracle or wonder. We shall tell the marvellous tale of how our bare cherry tree produced fruit in the middle of winter, and show this pudding as proof. How pleased he will be!'

They were about to rush off to King Arthur's court to present their pudding and tell the wonderful story, when Lady Cleges remembered something. She knew that Arthur would not accept any more gifts from them since they had become so poor. They would have to disguise themselves. That would be easy. As they no longer had any fine clothes, they didn't need to do much to what they were already wearing to appear to be poor peasants. Making sure that their faces were hidden in roomy hoods, they left for Camelot.

The delicious smell of the pudding wafted ahead, arriving just before them and making the guard's mouth water.

'What's your business? The King is already seated for the banquet and none may disturb him without good reason.'

'A present for the King, most fitting for his banquet.'

Seeing that the visitors were poor and humble, the guard thought that he could take advantage of them. How would they know how things worked at court?

'And what will you give me for letting you past this gate?'

Sir and Lady Cleges were shocked. It was the guard's duty to protect Arthur and his court, not to prevent guests from entering – and certainly not to use his position to ask for bribes, which is a dishonest way of getting money from people. The couple had a whispered conversation about what they should do. For once, Sir Cleges took his wife's advice.

He said, 'King Arthur will reward me for this gift. On my honour you shall have one third of what he gives me.'

The guard agreed and let them through, but the same thing happened at the inner gate, where the guard asked, 'What will you give me for letting you past this gate?'

'King Arthur will reward me for this gift. On my honour you shall have one third of what he gives me,' Sir Cleges said, and they were let through, but the same thing happened at the entrance to the Great Hall.

'What will you give me for letting you past this door?' the guard there asked.

'King Arthur will reward me for this gift. On my honour you shall have one third of what he gives me.'

As they entered the Great Hall, they noticed at once that people were looking rather gloomy. This was because everyone had been waiting a very long time to eat something, as nobody had a new miracle or wonder to tell to the court. As the scrumptious pudding smell spread through the room, loud gurgling noises came from people's tummies followed by wistful sighs as they eyed the pudding bowl. Their misery was especially unfortunate because it also happened to be Christmas Eve and everyone was too hungry by now to feel festive.

'Your Majesty, a wonder, a marvel I have to tell!' cried Sir Cleges.

'Thank goodness for that,' roared King Arthur, who had been out hunting all day and was ravenous.

The story of the miraculous cherry tree was told and the pudding was shared. Somehow, no matter how many there were to feed and no matter how small the pudding, there was enough for everyone. King Arthur was so delighted with the story and the pudding that he offered Sir Cleges any reward he could wish for.

'Twelve smacks with the flat of your sword, please, my King.'

'What kind of a reward is that? How can you ask for such a thing?'

It was then that Arthur was told about his dishonest guards and how they had been promised a third of any reward. If the promise were to be kept, this meant that each guard would receive four smacks and Sir Cleges none. King Arthur looked very serious when he heard how untrustworthy these guards were, but he also had to laugh when he realised how clever Lady Cleges' idea was. Except that he didn't know that it was Lady Cleges he was talking to. In fact, he didn't quite know who he was talking to.

'And who has honoured the court with such a fine wonder and gift?' he asked. 'I don't believe I know who I have been speaking to. What are your names?'

'If I might just see the reward I requested,' murmured Sir Cleges, backing away.

But Arthur was too quick for him. His sword, Excalibur, was out of its scabbard. Two silver thrusts, like the forked fangs of a serpent, hissed through the air and flicked back their hoods. Arthur recognised and embraced his old friends. He ordered the guards to come into the Great Hall and he smacked each of them four times with the flat

of his sword Excalibur. Then he took away the guards' weapons and ordered them to work with the pigs until they had learned better manners. They are probably still working in the pigsties to this day.

Knowing that his friend would still be too proud to accept any money, Arthur made Sir Cleges captain of the guard. This meant that no matter how generous he continued to be, at least he would have a good wage coming in every month. Lady Cleges was requested to make the marvellous pudding every year for their Christmas feast and it soon became known as Christmas pudding. Some people say that she kept the recipe secret and that it was only handed down from mother to daughter. If that's true, how come I was able to make it earlier? And is it something you are going to try to make at home?

How the Devil Shaped Somerset

Some people say that the Devil is a wicked creature with goats' horns on his head, which he sometimes tries to hide under a black silky top hat. He also has hooves like a goat which he sometimes tries to hide in shiny black shoes. Some people say that nobody knows what the Devil looks like, but he feels like that tiny worst bit in all of us that makes us squash snails and lie about eating the last piece of cake. Whichever you think, the Devil has always tried to make trouble for people and do as much harm as possible. Here are some stories about how his wicked deeds left their stony mark on the land of

Somerset, whether with bridges, islands, circles made of giant stones, or England's deepest gorge.

The Devil Digs Cheddar Gorge

The quiet little town of Cheddar really annoyed the Devil because people lived there so peacefully, happily making cheddar cheese and tending their apple orchards. He decided to ruin their lives by diverting the River Axe to flood their homes and wash them away. Further on lay the mighty Glastonbury Abbey, full of holy monks, bishops and abbots who, because they prayed all the time, made the Devil even angrier. He realised that he could wipe out both places at once if he caused the river to make enough of a splash.

The river ran mostly underground, and that annoyed the Devil too as he feared that it might get close enough to the fires of Hell to cool them down. He decided to solve all these problems in one go by digging right down through the huge rocky hills to the riverbed itself. Then he would dig a great channel through the hills which the water would pour down, drowning everything in its path. What a great idea – as long as you didn't live near Cheddar or Glastonbury or happen to be the giant Gorm.

What giant Gorm lacked in the way of brains he made up for in size. That is to say that he was hugely stupid. He only had one talent and that was for moving heaps of earth around, and giant-sized heaps of earth means hills. He had just about worked out that this required lots of digging and so he began. It happened that he started to dig close to where the Devil had started on his plan to change the course of the River Axe.

The Devil was surprised to hear an answering echo at each thrust of his spade. He stopped to listen. Muffled sounds of a spade continued, so it couldn't be an echo he was hearing. He went to investigate and saw that on the other side of the Mendip Hills, Gorm had made another chasm, a gash in the rocks which at the rate he was digging threatened to be bigger than his. The Devil was so jealous that he forgot his task and furiously hurled himself at Gorm.

The giant had enough sense to know that he should run. Unfortunately, he didn't have enough sense to realise that he would be a lot faster if he didn't try to take his latest load of earth with him. He lovingly balanced it on his spade so that none would fall off. At last he worked out that he would have to let it go if he wanted to escape the Devil, who was closing the gap between them. His dumped spadeful made a hill we now call Brent Knoll. Unfortunately, he then tripped over the hill he had just made. As he couldn't bear to entirely abandon that heap of earth, he tried to grab a handful as he fell. Gorm landed with a great splash in the Bristol Channel. Sadly, he had used up all his brain power by then, and didn't have the sense to get up, so

he drowned. His body became Brean Down and his outstretched right hand became Flat Holm, an island in the channel. As for his left hand, well that became Steep Holm, a lump of an island that looks like a clenched fist – because that was the hand that Gorm had clutched that last chunk of earth with.

So, in case you didn't already know, BIG is not the same as CLEVER! Yet we should be grateful to giant Gorm, because he distracted the Devil from his evil task of drowning the lovely towns of Cheddar and Glastonbury, which still produce delicious cheese, apple juice and Torsy Morsy cake to this day.

THE STONE
WEDDING

Not so long ago, many people used to think it was wrong to enjoy yourself on a Sunday and that you should have a quiet day praying, reading the bible and going to church. One Saturday, the Devil got to hear that there would be a wedding, and the thought of people being so happy made him grind his teeth with fury. He decided to lurk about to see if there would be a chance for him to make trouble.

The young bride was dizzy with happiness. After the service and the feast there was the dancing. As it was a beautiful June day, the dancing could take place outside. Round and round they danced in the long June evening, with the slanting sunlight and the lengthening shadows. The fiddler had played so long and hard that his fingers were numb, but the bride never seemed to tire. It was Midsummer, when we have the longest day and the shortest night. It is a magical time. It also happened to be a full moon, which is a magical time too.

The Devil knew that this was just the kind of over-excited atmosphere that can tip into tears, so he lurked in the shadows waiting for his chance. It was eleven o'clock at night, and the sky was still streaked with the last colours of sunset. The full moon shone brightly and there was plenty of light. Some of the guests had slipped away, but a few couples danced on. Then the clock struck midnight and the musician stopped playing. The bride was angry.

'How dare you stop playing in the middle of a dance? Have I not already told you that I will double your purse for playing into the night?'

'I have played into the night, Madam, and now that the clock has struck midnight it is the morning of the Sabbath day, our holy day of Sunday. Now is the time for praying, not for dancing, and I will play no more.'

The bride stamped her foot and tossed her head, but the fiddler put his instrument in its case and made for home. He hadn't gone far when he had to stop. It was as though his feet had become rooted to the ground. His head turned on his neck to angle itself to the sound of the sweetest music he had ever heard. Another fiddler had taken over where he had left off. His playing was so magical that the fiddler felt that his own was like a spade scraping on a stone. Where had this musician come from so late at night? Who could it be? Surely he knew all the best players in the district, and this music sounded like something from another world.

The fiddler crept back to the dancers and peered over a stone wall. There he saw the other musician, his shape a sliver of black in the silver moonlight, the shadows of the dancers long in the grass, flickering like black flames. He saw how the newcomer wore a very high top hat, he saw how he tapped his foot in time to the music, he saw how the moonlight lit up what were shaped more like hooves than shoes – and then he covered his ears and ran.

Next day the bride and groom and some of the wedding guests were nowhere to be found. In the field where they had been dancing, a circle made of huge stones could now be seen. The fiddler told everybody what he had seen and heard. Some people in the village said that the new musician was the Devil himself, who had turned the rest of the wedding party to stone as a punishment for dancing when they shouldn't. Some people said that had to be nonsense, that the fiddler must have been drunk, and that the newlyweds had run away with some of their friends. But that didn't explain how the stones had suddenly appeared, and it didn't explain how there were exactly as many stones as there were people who had disappeared.

A whole year after that, when it was Midsummer's Day once more, the fiddler returned to the stone circle. There was one stone, prouder looking than the others. The fiddler fashioned a wreath of wild flowers and, as it was June, it included the wild roses that grew along the wall where he had hidden. As he placed the flowers against the stone, the thorns must have scratched it because he saw some drops of blood appear at its base. Higher up, some clear drops ran down over the stony surface. When he tasted them, they were not sweet like dew, but salty like tears. You can try this yourself if you go to the Bridestone in the stone circle at Stanton Drew on Midsummer's Day.

THE DEVIL MAKES A SPLASH

We have heard how the Devil had been having such a good time causing trouble with stone: he had dug Britain's largest gorge and killed a giant; he had turned a wedding party into stone. Stone was great; it lasted almost forever and was a constant reminder of the harm that the Devil could do. Now it was time for some stone juggling.

The Devil chose his spot carefully for his next marvel. There was plenty of stone to use on Exmoor; it just needed a little rearranging. He chose a site near the village of Hawkridge, close to the fast-flowing River Barle. The long-suffering villagers lived near a river which ran so fast it wasn't safe to cross. It was too fast for fishing, sometimes even sweeping away their animals that drank from it. How they wished they had wings, like the hawks their village was named after. Then they would be able to fly across those dangerous waters instead of walking the long way round the valley.

One day they were astonished to hear a thunderous voice booming across the Barle Valley: 'I have come to make a bridge, you villagers of Hawkridge. Now see this…'

There was the Devil. Everyone recognised him from his top hat and pointy hooves. He seized a mighty slab of rock and twirled it on his fingertip. He launched it into the air and they watched as it came towards them, spinning slowly as it fell. Some ran this way, and some that way, thinking it would crush them. But the stone landed in the river, making such a splash that it could be heard as far away as Wales. Hypnotised, the villagers watched as the Devil juggled with three more:

Splish! Splash! Splish! Five times the Devil did this and finished as he had started, by spinning another stone on his fingertip. Then all was still, except for the rushing river. The fish had stopped leaping in surprise and the villagers were still watching, unblinking, with their mouths open. But the sound of the river was different, because now it was rushing under a perfectly formed, solid, safe bridge. Everyone was delighted, but not for long.

'Behold my bridge, and I mean MY bridge. The first being who dares to set a foot upon it will be destroyed by a thunderbolt. My flash of lightning will burn you to a crisp. You have been warned!'

And the Devil disappeared with a bang, a tongue of flame and a horrible smell. Around the valley echoed his shriek of evil laughter, splitting tree trunks and sending boulders rolling down the slopes, so nobody dared to use the bridge.

At last a very daring child stole her big brother's shoe. When she was at the edge of the bridge, she placed her own foot, still wearing its own shoe, inside her brother's huge one. She touched the edge of the bridge with the toe of her brother's shoe. But just as she placed it in position, she slipped her own shoe out of his. Out of nowhere came a lightning bolt and struck it. She was as quick as anyone could have been, but inside her own shoe, the tip of her big toe was blistered. Her brother's shoe, however, was a crisped and twisted piece of useless leather. The Devil's curse was proven to be true.

That night there was fish for dinner. Instead of eating hers, the child hid it in her pocket. Then she slipped away to where the local witch lived just outside the village. She was in luck: there was the witch's cat slinking about – a killer cat who killed for fun, snatched harmless bats out of the air, slunk into larders and stole. This was a cat who pretended to want you to stroke it and then turned on you with vicious scratches and bites. Now the fish was dangling at the end of a string. Now the string was attached to a stick. The cat followed the fish, the fish followed the string, the string

followed the stick and the stick followed the girl. All until they reached the Devil's bridge. Then there was a flick as the string leaped forward and the fish dangled over the great stones of the bridge.

That was not the cat's last supper. It didn't even reach the fish before a mighty flash of lightning struck it and it disappeared in a puff of smoke. The Devil had claimed his own, and not the kind of innocent mortal he had expected. Now that the curse was broken, the villagers joyfully used that bridge whenever they wanted. It is called Tarr Steps and you can visit it any time. The Devil won't be there because he is still ashamed at how he was outwitted by a mere girl with a fish. As for her brother, he always wondered how he had manged to lose that one shoe.

Part Four

Here Be Dragons

Blue Ben the Biggest

There seem to have been rather a lot of dragons in Somerset. One of them has even managed to get onto Somerset's flag.

Blue Ben was the biggest, or liked to think he was. Blue is a rather unusual colour for a Somerset dragon, but he wasn't always that colour. Before he became blue, he used to fly up and down where the River Severn touches the Somerset coast and tries to become the sea. This shoreline was his hunting ground. When he wasn't devouring people and animals, he was setting fire to everything. It was this love of arson that attracted the Devil's attention.

The Devil lived underground in Hell, where huge tunnels were filled with fire. That is where people who had been bad during their life on Earth were sent. There they were punished after their death, slowly roasting for the rest of forever. The Devil was jealous of Blue Ben's fire and wanted it for himself. He persuaded Ben to go and live with him in Hell by promising him an endless supply of barbecued humans to eat. In exchange for these, Ben's job was to keep the fires of Hell hotter than hot. He also had to pull a carriage full of the latest arrivals to their new homes in the fire-filled tunnels.

Both were happy with this arrangement, until the day when Ben overate himself. There had been a great battle between King Arthur and Saxon invaders which resulted in an extra supply of dead people. As it is rather hard to pretend that you have led a good life if your job has been to kill people, the Devil had his hands full. Blue Ben was extra busy distributing the wicked soldiers throughout their new fiery home and eating as many of them as possible.

Ben liked eating more than working. He figured out that the more people he ate, the fewer journeys he would have to make pulling that carriage full of newcomers. Because of the battle, there seemed no end of barbecued bodies. Ben ate and ate until his jaws ached and then he felt something he had never felt before, and that was FULL! All that food was stoking the fires that burned in his belly. Then Ben felt something else that he had never felt before and that was HOT! HOT! HOT!

There was a great streak of flame as Ben tore out of the tunnels of Hell and into the open air. Every blade of grass in Somerset was singed, the leaves turned to crisps and all the sheep turned black. There was a terrible smell of burning hair as people's eyebrows burned off. Ben plunged into the Severn Sea to cool down. A huge cloud of steam arose, covering the whole of the coast and rolling inland like a bank of fog. It lasted for days, blotting out the sun and covering the land in a kind of twilight.

What Ben hadn't thought about was that where the Severn joins the sea are some of the largest tides in the world. These also help to make it one of the muddiest places in the world – a particularly sticky blue-grey mud. Ben was especially heavy after all he had eaten. He got stuck in the mud and began to sink. Meanwhile the tides came and went, came and went. Each time the tide came in Ben was covered in a layer of sticky mud, each time the tide went out the dragon's heat hardened the mud to stone. Every layer made Ben look bluer and bluer. Eventually the cool waters put out the dragon's fire and the clouds of steam blew away. Then the people found a new feature on their coastline: Somerset's first and only blue dragon, set in stone. You can see Blue Ben to this day when the tide goes out, if you know where to look, just past a sign that says 'Beware of the Mud', and now you know why.

King Arthur's Dragon

The new king, Arthur Pendragon, had many enemies. He had to win over powerful warlords to his side. He also had to defend the island of Britain from the pirates and slave traders who sailed up the Bristol Channel and landed on the Somerset coast. There they burned everything they didn't steal and killed everyone they didn't enslave.

King Arthur was riding along the coast where another king, King Catho, ruled, hoping to make friends and to persuade him to join forces against the Danish pirates. Ahead was King Catho's fortified settlement on the top of a hill, but Arthur was riding through flat, muddy marshland. All seemed dull and wet and grey. It was hard to tell where the grey mud became the grey beach, where the grey beach became the grey sea, where the grey sea became the grey sky. It was raining so heavily that it was hard to tell which was the wetter – land or sea or sky. That was why it was strange to smell burning. The closer Arthur rode to the castle, the stronger the smell became, and he thought he could see smudges of black amongst the grey.

King Catho looked at his visitor and wondered. So they were true, these rumours of a young king who had appeared out of nowhere, born through Merlin's magic. Merlin, the most powerful magician in the land, had created a High King to rule over all the kings of the island of Britain. There stood Arthur, shivering, covered in mud, wet hair dripping into his eyes, a most un-kingly sight. When Catho heard about Arthur's mission, he said, 'I'll help you if you'll help me.'

'Anything you ask,' replied the foolish young king.

Catho smiled secretly into his beard before telling Arthur that the help he needed was to be rid of the dragon that had been devastating the area, burning crops, devouring animals and people.

'Rather like the Danish pirates,' said Arthur, and the two men knew that they could be friends. But first there was the little matter of Arthur promising to get rid of a rather powerful dragon. How on earth or sea or sky was he going to do that? No point in getting too comfortable with a hot meal and dry clothes, Arthur set off at once to get the impossible over and done with. As he rode along he thought how foolish he was to make a promise he had no way of keeping.

The louder splashing of his horse's hooves made him realise that he was riding on the beach where the waves met the shore. There on that expanse of heaving grey, he saw a warm glow. A rosy wedge of colour which seemed to trap all the colours of the sunrise and sunset was floating towards him. Stranger still, the grey clouds parted and a shaft of golden sunlight lit up the curious object. How it sparkled in the sudden sunlight! Through the dazzle, Arthur could see that it was carved with signs and symbols of the new religion. There were Christian crosses, doves and saints' heads with halos round them. What a beautiful object it was, bobbing towards him on the tide, strange and yet somehow familiar.

When the waves brought it to the grey sand, Arthur dismounted to pull it clear of the water. As he grasped it, he was astonished to feel that it was made of stone. How could something so heavy have been floating on the surface of the water? Grunting with the effort, he heaved it up the beach so that the tide couldn't wash it away again. Then he decided that he couldn't leave such a precious object unprotected. The best he could do would be to hide it with seaweed.

He was so busy gathering up the slippery stuff that he didn't notice how nervously his horse was behaving. At first the breaking of the waves had muffled the sound of angry hissing. By the time Arthur heard it, his horse had bolted. From the grey gloom of the marshes there came snaking towards him the most enormous dragon. Arthur was trapped between monster and sea. He stood there staring, not able to believe what his eyes were showing him, until he turned and fled up the beach.

Covered in mud and sweat, blinded by salt spray, his sword making him stumble at every other step, the High King of All the Britons staggered and gasped his way along the beach with the dragon following him. Then he blundered into someone and fell over. He heard a man's voice say, 'I wonder whether you have found my altar? It should have washed up on this beach by now, but I can't seem to find it.'

So that's what Arthur had found! Of course, he realised now that it had reminded him of the altar in the church where he had been crowned king. He could see the lumbering shape of the dragon drawing closer. He spat out a mouthful of gritty sand: 'I'll help you if you'll help me,' he squeaked.

'Certainly, my king,' came the reply, and the holy man Carantoc took from around his neck the strip of silk that he wore, to show that he was a man of the Church. He pointed his staff at the dragon, who was by now so close that its fiery breath had dried up all the mud that covered Arthur.

'Sit,' commanded Carantoc. The dragon sat.

'Stay,' commanded Carantoc. The dragon stayed while the holy man tied the silk round the monster's neck like a leash.

'Your altar is back this way. I covered it with seaweed to protect it,' stammered Arthur.

'How thoughtful of you. Heel,' came the command, to the dragon, not the king.

The young man and the old walked back along the beach together, the dragon waddling alongside. Arthur showed where the altar had been disguised with seaweed.

'Let it stay there for now,' said Carantoc. As the three walked along the beach, back towards the castle, the holy man told Arthur the story of how he and his altar had come to be there. He had been a hermit, spending a life of prayer living in a cave on the other side of the channel in the land of Wales. One night a dream told him to carve an altar and put it out to sea. Even though it would be made of stone it would float on water through the power of prayer. Wherever the altar landed he was to build a church, a shrine to celebrate the new Christian religion. He had walked along the Welsh coast until he had found that beautiful lump of rock. Perhaps it had washed up from the English side. He had carved it, floated it and followed it in his boat, and Arthur knew the rest.

As they approached the castle, Arthur said, 'Would you mind awfully if I took a turn at leading the dragon for a bit? You see, there was this foolish promise…'

'No need to explain, my king, certainly you may lead the dragon,' and Arthur knew that he had made another friend.

Catho was delighted because the dragon was no longer going to be a threat. Arthur was delighted because Catho gave him plenty of soldiers to fight off the Danes. Carantoc was delighted because Catho also gave him money to build his church. Arthur's horse was delighted because the tamed dragon had become vegetarian. The castle gardener was delighted because the dragon only ate seaweed. The cooks were delighted because they never needed to worry about the kitchen fires going out. The ladies of the court were delighted because they had something to warm their feet on.

Then, because it was so much easier to think when he wasn't covered in mud, the High King Arthur had an idea. He put the dragon to patrol up and down the shore to scare off the Danish pirates. The dragon was delighted because it could be scary again and get plenty of exercise. The Danes were not delighted because they had to abandon their plans to invade. They also felt rather foolish because the prows of their ships had wooden dragon heads on to scare off enemies. However, these only attracted the real dragon, so they were the ones who ended up terrified.

With a tame dragon protecting that part of the coast, the soldiers were free to take on other enemies. The story being told was that it had been Arthur who had tamed the dragon, and Carantoc let him take the glory. Well, wasn't the High King's name 'Arthur Pendragon', which means 'Dragon's Head', and didn't that just prove it? His reputation spread, more and more people flocked to his side, and Arthur became the most popular king that Britain has ever known.

Somewhere on this beautiful island he lies sleeping with his knights under a great hill. Many places claim to be his resting place, including Cadbury Castle in Somerset. Perhaps he smiles in his sleep every Beltane, every May Eve, when people celebrate that festival with their dancing, prancing hobby horse, which they pull up from the shore at Minehead. In the whole country that is the only one with a body shaped like a boat and a head shaped like a dragon.

A Dragon Halved

Not so long ago, Somerset used to be full of dragons. Most of them made a real nuisance of themselves, eating all the cattle and sheep. When those had all gone, they started on the humans. If they couldn't find any, they breathed out fire so everything got burned.

One such dragon had its den amongst the Quantock Hills. Any surviving people were too frightened to go up there, but why would they want to, when there were no sheep left to graze and the woods that provided firewood had been burnt?

There was just one old woman who was still keen to climb up into those hills. Every year, just as summer was turning into autumn, she would climb to the top to collect whortleberries. These are a kind of blueberry, a tiny delicious fruit that tastes like all the flavours of summer in one bite. Creeping Annie would toil up those hills and fill her baskets. She would crawl down again when she couldn't cram in another one of those blue-bright berries. Coming down was even slower than going up, because of the weight of those huge baskets. She looked like some giant hermit crab that had strayed inland from the Severn Sea – that's why she was called Creeping Annie.

When she had collected her crop of whortleberries, she would boil them up in her tiny cottage and turn them into jam. Some she stored in jars for the winter but most went into the tarts and pies that she sold at a nearby fair. She had been doing this for so long, and was such an expert, that many came to that fair just to buy what she had baked.

As she was cooking, the delicious smells that came from her kitchen would bring the wild animals out of hiding, clustering at her back door. Birds would circle above her chimney and the house mice would jostle to be first in the queue at the mouse holes.

However, now that she was so old, gathering whortleberries had become much harder. With old age, her bent back had set into the curve those heavy baskets had shaped. Her legs had bowed and bandied so that Creeping Annie looked even more crab-like than ever. As the berry-picking time drew near, she didn't want to admit that she couldn't climb those hills because she was too old. Now there was another problem. A dragon-shaped problem. She didn't want to admit that she was frightened of a dragon either. What to do?

Creeping Annie had noticed that there was still one green slope that hadn't been burnt by the dragon's fiery breath, so the whortleberry bushes would still be unharmed. But the dragon could be lurking anywhere and must be very hungry by now. She knew that the next day would be perfect weather for picking and that she had to seize her chance. The night before, she made everything ready for an early start.

As she set off in the early morning, her old dog started to bark, and he only did that for strangers. Annie wondered who it could be, as there had been no more visitors since the dragon had made those hills his home. She easily made herself seem part of the hedge with those huge baskets on her back. The man strode whistling past without noticing her. From the axe in his belt and the width of his arms, it was clear that he was a woodcutter.

When he had gone past a bend in the track, she threw herself in the ditch and started to cry out: 'Oh me! Oh misery me! What is the world come to when a young man will pass an old woman by without offering a helping hand. And her so weak and him so strong, Oh misery me!'

Annie paused a moment to listen out for the sound of returning footsteps. She was not disappointed when she heard the woodcutter hurrying back.

'Oh misery me! Am I to die here in this ditch, helpless like a topsy-turvy crab? A moment is all it would take to pull me rightwise up, but there's no kindness left in this sad world…'

She felt a grip strong as badgers' jaws, then arms strong as young oaks lifting her. Massive hands like sails were flapping at her, brushing leaves and dirt from her clothes, so that she nearly fell back into the ditch.

'There now, Missus, be you steady yet?'

But Creeping Annie was not steady. She flung herself on the ground, weeping and wailing and almost crushing her baskets as she thrashed and rolled to and fro.

'Steady, he asks! Where's the use in being steady when an old woman, all alone in the world, will starve this coming winter!'

He helped her up again and she allowed him to guide her to a nearby tree stump. There she sat and told him that falling into the ditch had so shaken and bruised her that she would not be able to climb the hill to fill her baskets. If she couldn't gather whortle-berries she would have nothing to sell at the fair. If she had nothing to sell she wouldn't have enough money to survive…

The kind young man explained that he had come from a distant village and was looking for work. He had heard that a woodcutter was needed at a big estate beyond the hills. It would be no trouble to take her baskets up the slopes and gather berries for her. If she waited for him at the bottom of the hill he could be back later, return her filled baskets, and be on his way.

Creeping Annie could not believe her luck. Here was a generous man who had come from so far away that he hadn't even heard of the dragon. To make sure that he was able to keep his strength up, she gave him the packed lunch and bottle of cider she had prepared earlier. Then she dozed in the late summer sun, thinking how pleasant it was to sit there without her old legs aching or a hungry dragon breathing down her neck.

Meanwhile the man had climbed the hill, filling Annie's baskets with whortleberries as he went. On the other side of the valley he noticed the burned slopes and, being a woodsman, wondered at the charred remains of the trees.

'Must have powerful strong storms in these parts,' he thought. 'Must have been a gurt lashing of lightning to burn all they trees down to their stumps.'

He was at the top and the baskets were full. Time to have a rest amongst the greenery and the bushes whose fruit he would have to leave. It was so overgrown that it took a while for him to find a log to sit on and eat the lunch he had been given.

As he was munching away, he thought the log shifted beneath him. He resettled his weight and continued chewing. Despite this, he felt the log rolling slightly. He planted his feet more firmly but the log rolled the other way. It was a very strange thing for a log to do. He was a woodcutter and he should know.

'Keep still while I am eating,' he cried, and slapped the rough surface of the wood.

The log did not keep still and that was because it wasn't a log, it was a rather large dragon that had been woken up by being sat on. The woodcutter felt his seat ripple beneath him, almost tipping him into some nettles.

'Keep still I tell 'ee. Don't 'ee have no manners?'

Annoyed, he seized the axe from his belt and gave the log a mighty chop. He was so strong that his axe cut all the way through with one blow. He had chopped the dragon in half! Still believing that he had cut into a fallen trunk he only realised his mistake when he saw it move off in opposite directions – one half showing the dragon's tail and back legs, the other showing front legs and a fire-breathing head. Horrified, he watched for a moment as the two halves crept and crawled away. Then he ran. The other surprise was that he thought to pick up Annie's baskets as he fled.

He arrived much sooner than expected. Annie was delighted to see how much fruit he had gathered. He was less than delighted when telling her about the dragon.

'How could 'ee have sent me up there knowing that I could meet such a creature?' he asked.

'How was I to know they stories about that dragon was real?' she replied. 'Dragons is only

in fairy tales. It's a long time since I believed in they,' cackled Creeping Annie, thinking how long it had been since she was a child.

She thanked him for his efforts and the woodcutter went on his way. It was only when he was on the far side of the Quantock Hills that he wondered how Annie could have failed to notice those burnt slopes. How could she have explained them to herself?

Meanwhile Annie was busy preparing for the fair. As she sold her tarts and pies she told everyone how she had sent the woodcutter up into the hills to kill the dragon. Curious villagers followed the trail and found the place where it had happened: there was the ground gouged with a gash from the axe blow. There were the brambles and nettles withered from the poisonous dragon blood. Creeping Annie was now a heroine and the villagers made sure that she was always well provided for from that time on.

Before long, tales came back to the village of people seeing different dragon halves. Some saw the tail end and some saw the head end. Fortunately, these were always described as crawling in opposite directions. That's another reason to always close gates if you are in the countryside. We don't want those halves finding each other and joining up!

The riddle: The more often you give me away, the longer you keep me. What am I?

. . . .

The answer: 'A story', because you give it away by telling it and the more you tell it, the more it stays in your memory.

The destination for history
www.thehistorypress.co.uk